says,
"Please
and
Thank You"

PUFFIN BOOKS

Dear Parents

This book represents the use of polite expressions "please" and "thank you" within a fun story. Young children learn manners best through modelling – Barney always tries to set a good example for young children. You can help to reinforce understanding of the use of "please" and "thank you" by encouraging your child to respond with the correct word as you read the story.

We consider books to be lifelong gifts that develop and enhance the love of reading. When your child sees you reading – whether it's a book, magazine or newspaper – you are modelling the value of reading. We hope you and your child enjoy reading along with Barney and Baby Bop!

Mary Ann Dudko, Ph.D.
Margie Larsen, M.Ed.
Early Childhood Educational Specialists

PUFFIN BOOKS

Published by the Penguin Group under licence from Lyons Partnership, L.P.
Penguin Books Ltd, 27 Wrights Lane, London W8 5TZ, England
Penguin Books USA Inc., 375 Hudson Street, New York, New York 10014, USA
Penguin Books Australia Ltd, Ringwood, Victoria, Australia
Penguin Books Canada Ltd, 10 Alcorn Avenue, Toronto, Ontario, Canada M4V 3B2
Penguin Books (NZ) Ltd, 182–190 Wairau Road, Auckland 10, New Zealand

Penguin Books Ltd, Registered Offices: Harmondsworth, Middlesex, England

First published in the USA by Barney™ Publishing, a division of Lyons Partnership, L.P. 1994
Published in Puffin Books 1995
20 19 18 17 16 15 14

Barney™ says, "Please and Thank You"

Written by Stephen White

Illustrated by Rick Grayson

"We're going to have a party,"
says Baby Bop.
"It's Mr Bear's make-believe birthday!"

"Oh, a party sounds like fun," says Barney.
"And we can practise using good manners."

"What are manners?" Baby Bop asks. "Manners are special ways to be nice to other people," Barney tells her.

"One way to show good manners is to say '**please**' and '**thank you**'," Barney says.

"Let's try now,"
Barney says happily.
"Baby Bop, will you get
some party dishes...
please?"

Baby Bop brings lots
of party dishes.
Barney says,
"Thank you, Baby Bop."

Baby Bop says,
"Barney, will you blow up
some party balloons...**please**?"
"I'll be happy to,"
answers Barney.
Barney blows up all
the balloons.
Baby Bop says,
"**Thank you**, Barney."

"Now let's make party snacks for Mr Bear," says Barney. "Baby Bop, will you get the peanut butter...**please**?"

"Yes, I will," laughs Baby Bop.
Baby Bop gets a big jar
of peanut butter.

Baby Bop and Barney take turns making yummy sandwiches. Barney says, "May I eat my sandwich now...**please**?"

Baby Bop says, "Yes, you may."
Barney doesn't say anything after
that...because his mouth is full!
But after he chews and
swallows, he says,
"**Thank you**, Baby Bop."

"Mr Bear would like some party music,"
says Baby Bop.
"Barney, will you make some music…**please**?"

"Yes, I will," laughs Barney.
Barney makes lots of happy music.
Crash-bang-boom!
Baby Bop says,
"**Thank you**, Barney."

Barney says, "Baby Bop, would you put on a puppet show for Mr Bear…**please**?"

Barney claps his hands for Baby Bop's wonderful puppet show.
Barney says,
"**Thank you**, Baby Bop."

"Now Mr Bear wants to take a train ride,"
says Baby Bop.
"Barney, will you drive the train…**please**?"

"Here we go," Barney laughs,
"*Chugga-chugga, woo-woooo!*"
Baby Bop says,
"**Thank you**, Barney."

When the train stops, Baby Bop puts her toys away.
"I hope you had fun at your party,"
Baby Bop says to Mr Bear.
"Barney, will you help me clean
the party dishes…**please**?"

"Of course I will,"
says Barney.
Baby Bop says,
"**Thank you**, Barney."

The two friends take turns
washing and drying dishes.
Barney says, "**Thank you** for inviting
me to your nice party, Baby Bop."
Baby Bop smiles happily.
"You're welcome," she says.